This edition published by Parragon Books Ltd in 2015

Parragon Books Ltd
Chartist House
15–17 Trim Street
Bath BA1 1HA, UK
www.parragon.com

ISBN 978-1-4723-9111-7

Visit www.disney.com/fairies

Printed in China

Bath • New York • Cologne • Melbourne • Delhi
Hong Kong • Shenzhen • Singapore • Amsterdam

One beautiful day in Pixie Hollow, Rosetta, Silvermist and Iridessa were planting sunflowers when Zarina walked past.
"Hey, Zarina! Out of pixie dust again?" asked Rosetta.
Fairies use pixie dust to fly, but Zarina preferred to walk.
"Just out for a stroll. You know me!" replied Zarina.

Zarina was a dust-keeper fairy and, one day, it was her turn to pour the special Blue Pixie Dust into the Pixie Dust Tree.

Mixing Blue Pixie Dust with golden pixie dust made the gold dust multiply!

But the head dustkeeper warned her, "Dust-keepers are forbidden to tamper with pixie dust."

But secretly Zarina had been saving up her pixie dust. After finding a speck of Blue Dust in her hair, Zarina was inspired to try one of her many failed pixie-dust experiments again, this time adding a tiny bit of the Blue Dust speck. The gold dust turned orange!

Zarina shared her discovery with her friend Tinker Bell – the new orange dust allowed Zarina to bend a moonbeam.

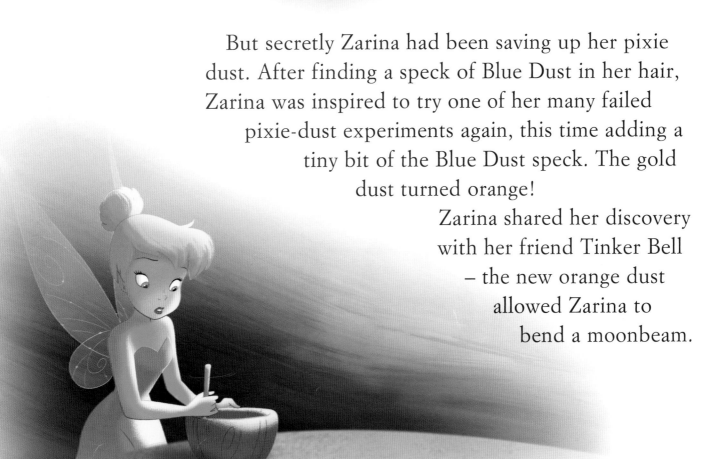

Zarina wanted to experiment more! Tink was worried.
"I really think you should stop," she said firmly.

Zarina turned and accidentally bumped into a plant,
spilling all of her new pink dust on it. The plant's vines
grew quickly, spreading all over Pixie Hollow.

Zarina couldn't believe the damage! When Fairy Gary saw the pink dust, he knew Zarina had been experimenting with pixie dust. He told Zarina she could no longer be a dust-keeper fairy.

She was upset. She rushed back home, packed her things and left Pixie Hollow.

One year later, the fairies celebrated the
Four Seasons Festival.

While Periwinkle dazzled the crowd at the
amphitheatre with her ice-skating skills, Tink
and her friends were backstage working on
their act for the show.

As everyone watched Periwinkle's
performance, Tinker Bell saw
a fairy sprinkling pink dust
behind the crowd.

"Wait. Is that ...
Zarina?" asked Tink.

Suddenly, flowers sprouted in the amphitheatre – and then they burst open and sprayed pollen into the air. Rosetta knew it would make everyone fall asleep.

After Tink and her friends came out of hiding to protect themselves from the pollen, they discovered the Blue Pixie Dust was missing!

They followed its blue glow to a rowing boat where they saw Zarina showing the bag of dust to pirates. Tinker Bell assumed the pirates had made Zarina take the dust.

But then the fairies watched in shock as a pirate called James said to Zarina, "Let me say, your plan worked perfectly ... Captain."

The fairies rescued the bag of Blue Pixie Dust from the pirates and flew away from the boat.

"Give me back that dust!" shouted Zarina as she chased after them.

She threw multicoloured dust at them, knocking them through a waterfall and out cold. Zarina took back the bag of Blue Pixie Dust and flew off.

When the fairies woke up they discovered that the dust had swapped their talents and their outfits!

The fairies used their new talents to find the pirate ship that Zarina had been taking the Blue Pixie Dust to. They sneaked aboard.

The ship sailed to Skull Rock where, inside a cave, Zarina had grown a Pixie Dust Tree. The pirates wanted the pixie dust from the tree to make their ship fly! Some of the fairies sneaked into Zarina's cabin, where they listened to James and Zarina's plans. The others tried to listen from outside.

James watched Zarina preparing the Blue Pixie Dust. "So the secret is to put the Blue Dust directly into the tree. Very impressive, Captain!"

Zarina and James made their way to the tree, which was inside Skull Rock. Slowly, Zarina started to tip the container of Blue Dust into the dust well of the tree. Then she saw the fairies.

Zarina drew her sword and called to her pirate friends, who caught the fairies in nets.

"Zarina, don't do this! Come back home," begged Tinker Bell.

"I'll never go back to Pixie Hollow," answered Zarina. "This is exactly where I belong."

Tink and the others were captured by the pirates and taken to the galley, where the ship's cook put them in an old crab cage. The fairies tried their best to escape, but they were locked up tight.

Meanwhile, Zarina added Blue Pixie Dust to the tree, which then started to make golden dust flow. The pirates cheered! Zarina sprinkled it on James.

She taught him to fly and they soared through the
air together. But when they landed back on the ship,
James locked Zarina in a lantern. Now that he had the
dust, he didn't need Zarina – he had never been her
friend, afterall.

The fairies finally managed to free themselves and helped Zarina escape from the lantern.

Zarina apologized and offered to help stop the pirates. Suddenly, they realized that if they used their talents together they could defeat them.

Fawn used her new light talent to shoot scorching light-beams down at the pirates. Silvermist, now a fast-flying fairy, created a whirlwind to knock the ship off course.

While Zarina and James fought, the ship started to tip
over. James clung to the mast, trying not to fall into the sea.
Zarina took the vial of Blue Pixie Dust that he had round
his neck. When he saw the golden pixie dust
start to fall from the ship into the sea he
reached for it and fell!

But then James, covered in golden dust, flew up behind
Zarina. He took the vial of Blue Pixie Dust back from her,
spilling a speck. "Take it. What's one speck between friends?"
he said.

Zarina threw the speck at him. "No, you should have it all!"

The speck of Blue Pixie Dust made the gold dust that was
on James multiply and he flew wildly through the air before
plunging into a giant wave!

The fairies congratulated each other on defeating the pirates and turned the ship round.

Zarina gave the vial of Blue Pixie Dust to Tink. "Please take this back to Pixie Hollow," she said.

But Tink was not going to return without her friend.

"Zarina, we didn't come just for the Blue Pixie Dust," said Tink, smiling.

Zarina, Tink and the other fairies flew the
ship back to Pixie Hollow where Zarina used her
dust to wake up everyone in the amphitheatre.
Tink told them how Zarina had created
different types of pixie dust and grown
another Pixie Dust Tree.

Queen Clarion asked Zarina for a
demonstration of her talent so she
changed the fairies' talents back
to normal.

Everyone was very happy that
Zarina had come back home!